Lech Bledowski

I was surprised how hard it is to get a job here so I can support my family. I knew I would not be able to be a lawyer right away because we have Roman law in Poland as opposed to the common law system you have in the United States. I was willing to take any job to feed my wife and three children, but it is impossible to live on minimum wage, even when we both work. Here in Tidewater, five dollars an hour is considered good pay—but it's not nearly enough to get out of poverty. It is hard on a man when he can't support his family. I hope when I've been here five years and get my citizenship, I can get a job doing legal work and translation for immigrants and refugees. Right now my future is a big question mark. It's really a problem to have no recommendations. It helps to have connections. We are totally unconnected. All I have is my résumé and my willingness to work. I knew the streets weren't paved with gold here, but I still was not prepared for how difficult it would be to give my family food and shelter. I don't like taking food stamps. I did not come here to live on charity. I was a lawyer in my country for twelve years before I came here, so I was used to a certain standard of living and place in the community. I want to make a life for my family here similar to what I left behind. I didn't come here to be a millionaire, I emigrated because the Communists made me unwelcome in Poland.

There is a lot to get used to when you immigrate. For example, the casualness of friendships is very different than in Eastern Europe. Here people are very friendly, but they don't really take much responsiblity in their relationships. Americans are not nearly so interested in politics as Europeans because for the most part they have comfortable lives. I hope that one day my family will be comfortable too. I truly believe that a hardworking person has a chance to make a good life for himself, but you have to be able to sell yourself here. No matter how impressive your experience may be, if you don't have the skills to go out in the world and promote yourself, you don't have as much of a chance as the person who can really market himself. This is not easy for me or my wife, even though we have many years of professional experience in Poland. We have to learn to be more American and sell ourselves. It's hard to have a lot of confidence if your English is not so good, but what can I do but believe in myself? This is my life, I can't give up.

Now that I've been here four years, I have a much more realistic view of democracy. I always had a romantic idea about the system when I was behind the Iron Curtain. The pluses are very real, but so are the minuses. Even knowing the weaknesses firsthand, I would not presume to change it. In the long run it works better than anything else civilization has been able to devise so far. I'm free to fail here, but I'm also free to succeed, and I believe I ultimately will.